Mermaid Mysteries

Melody
and the
Sea Dragon

First published in Great Britain in 2012
by Boxer Books Limited.
www.boxerbooks.com

Library of Congress Cataloging-in-Publication Data

Kit, Katy.
Melody and the sea dragon / by Katy Kit ; illustrated by Tom Knight.
p. cm.—(Mermaid mysteries ; 4)
Summary: Coral, Jasmine, Rosa, and Sula help recover a missing chest of
jewels, and Melody appeals to King Nepture on behalf of the falsely accused
and banished sea dragon, in time for all to enjoy the spring festivities.
ISBN 978-0-8075-5082-3 (hardcover)—ISBN 978-0-8075-5083-0 (pbk.)
[1. Mermaids—Fiction. 2. Dragons—Fiction. 3. Fairies—Fiction. 4.
Magic—Fiction.] I. Knight, Tom, ill. II. Title.
PZ7.K67119Me 2012
[Fic]—dc23
2011034172

ISBN: 978-0-8075-5082-3 (hardcover)
ISBN: 978-0-8075-5083-0 (paperback)

10 9 8 7 6 5 4 3 2 1 LB 15 14 13 12

For more information about Albert Whitman & Company,
visit our web site at www.albertwhitman.com.

Mermaid
Mysteries

Melody
and the
Sea Dragon

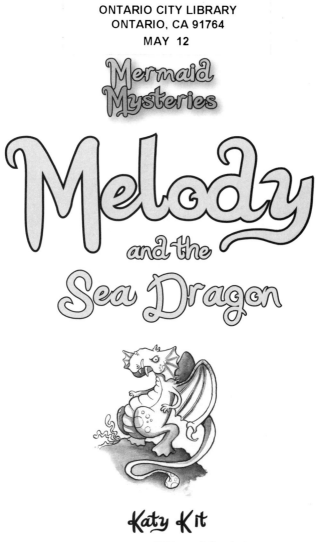

Katy Kit

Illustrated by **Tom Knight**

Albert Whitman & Company
Chicago, Illinois

Contents

CHAPTER 1

Dressing Up

"Ruby, sapphire, diamond, emerald, opal, pearl," said Melody, pointing one-by-one at the gemstones that were laid out on the seabed in front of her. The five mermaid friends had gathered out at Coral Reef to make

clothes and jewelry for the Mermaid
Bay Spring Ball. Surrounded by
fields full of silky seaweed, dainty sea
pods, sparkling sea stars, and golden
seagrass, it was the perfect place to
spend an afternoon.

"What about
this one,
Melody?"
asked
Rosa,
picking
up a clear
blue stone and
holding it up to the light.

"That's aquamarine," replied Melody, pushing her glasses back on her nose. "It's called that because it's the color of seawater. In Latin, *aqua* means water and *marine* is just another word for sea."

"Latin? What's that? You're so clever, Melody," said Rosa. "How do you know all these things? All I know is that it will make a wonderful necklace. Will you

hold this strand of silver seaweed,
please, so that I can tie it in place?"

Melody held the delicate strand
while Rosa threaded the gemstone on.

"There . . ." she said, holding it up.
"Perfect!"

All the mermaids were skilled

at making jewelry, and they loved dressing up. The Spring Ball gave them the perfect excuse.

"Do you remember last year's ball?" said Jasmine. "Myrtle and Muriel were determined to arrive in style, so they persuaded a dolphin to pull their carriage. It swam at top speed and took a shortcut

through
Five Fathom
Forest.
When they
arrived,
Myrtle's top
was torn to
tatters and
Muriel's tiara
was bent out of
shape. They thought everyone was
laughing at them. They were furious
for weeks."

Myrtle and Muriel were two older
mermaids. They were always being

mean to the five younger mermaids, who tried to keep out of their way.

"So how are we going to get there?" said Coral.

"We could use some mermaid magic to create a few water ponies," said Rosa, "and harness them to giant clamshells."

"That's a good idea," said Sula. "I'll round up some sea horses tomorrow."

"I'm so excited," said Coral. "I've never been to a ball before."

"That's right," said Jasmine. "You weren't here last year, were

you? Oh, it's such fun. It's held out at
Watery Downs."

"Is there dancing?" asked Coral.

"Plenty," replied Jasmine. "Throughout the whole afternoon. The last dance is the best one though: It's called 'Weave the Weed.'"

"That is a very strange name," giggled Coral.

"It's a strange dance!" joked Jasmine. "Everyone brings a string of seaweed onto which they've threaded jewels. When the dance is called, everyone who wants to join in stands in one

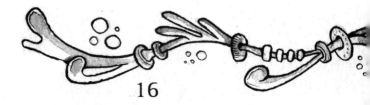

of four lines of dancers that together form a square. Then the music begins, and the dancers swim across the square to the other side, weaving their weed first over then under everyone else's as they go. They do this over and over again until a huge seaweed carpet is woven. That's why it's called 'Weave the Weed.'"

"Sounds difficult," said Coral.

"You can get a little tied up, but it's great fun," continued Jasmine.

"Afterward the carpet is laid on the seabed and covered with the most delicious food. It's then that the feast begins."

"Weave the Weed is a very old dance," said Melody. "Long ago, before we were born, after all the food had been eaten, the carpet was rolled up each year and given to the sea dragon to take back to his lair. That was before the water fairies put a spell on him and banished him to the underwater caves behind Rainbow Falls. Since then, the carpets have been given to King Neptune to use in the palace."

"Why was the sea dragon banished?" asked Rosa.

"Because he got greedy," said Melody. "Apparently he started stealing things from the mermaids' homes. Then, one day, a mermaid went missing . . ."

The mermaids gasped.

"And the sea dragon was blamed," she continued.

"What a frightening story," said Sula. "Thank goodness he's not going to be at the ball this year."

"Oh, it's going to be such fun," said Rosa. "Only two more days to wait!"

"What do you think of this?" said Jasmine. She held up a strapless top. It was covered in hundreds of tiny seed pearls.

"It's stunning!" exclaimed Coral. The other mermaids agreed.

"And incredibly precious," said

Melody.
"Especially
when you
think that
every one

of those tiny pearls took around two
years to grow!"

"Just how do you know so many
facts, Melody?" asked Rosa. "You seem
to know something about everything."

Melody glowed. She liked people
to think she was clever and loved
nothing more than telling people
what she knew.

"I'm interested in things, and

I've got a good memory," she boasted.

"Well, I'm very impressed," said Rosa. "I'm too tired to think of anything right now."

think of anything right now."

"Yes, it's getting late. We should go back," said Melody. "We can come for a couple of hours tomorrow after school to finish up. Put everything back in the chest, then I'll lock it and hide it behind these sea fans.

The chest is really heavy, so we'll all
need to push it to get it to move."

CHAPTER 2

Moon-Bathing

The following afternoon, as soon as school was over, the five mermaids set out on the short trip back to Coral Reef. They chattered excitedly as they swam.

"There's a full moon this evening,"

said Sula. "I thought that if there's time later, we could go moon-bathing."

The mermaids' eyes lit up. Sometimes, when the moon was full, the young mermaids would wait until evening when the beaches of Mermaid Bay were empty, swim to the shore, and flip their bodies out onto the sand. There they would lie, stretching out their long tails and soaking up the moonlight. Moon-bathing was a real treat.

"What a fantastic idea," said Jasmine. "The perfect way to relax after a busy afternoon."

"Well, we'd better get a move on, then," said Rosa. "Come on, everyone. Hurry up!"

The five mermaids finned as fast as firefish. Rosa reached Coral Reef first. She swam over to where they had left the chest. "It's gone!" she exclaimed.

"It can't be," said Melody. "It's too heavy. It took all our strength to push it over the seabed yesterday."

"Well, it is," said Rosa. "Come and take a look for yourself."

Melody swam over. Sure enough, the chest wasn't there. She started

looking around for clues right away.
Soon, she spotted something sticking
out of the seabed. She picked it up.
"Look. It's a scale."

The other mermaids gathered around.

"But it's not a mermaid scale," said Melody. "It's the wrong shape. Mermaid scales are the shape of teardrops; this one's round."

"And look at the coral around here," said Jasmine. "It's broken."

Sure enough, a large area of coral had been snapped off, as if something or someone had sat on it. Then Sula noticed something else. "What's this?" she asked.

The others swam over. Sula held up a long, thin white tube with lots of

soft, hairy strands sticking out of it. At one end, the strands stuck together to form a point. The mermaids shrugged their shoulders. Even Melody had never seen anything like it before.

Just then, Myrtle and Muriel swam

up, carrying bundles of golden seagrass.
"What are you five up to?" said Myrtle.
"Weren't you going to spend the
afternoon decorating your dresses for
the Spring Ball?"

"That's why we're here," said Jasmine.

"Well, where are they?" asked Muriel, looking around.

"We're not too sure," said Sula. "They seem to have gone missing."

"Missing!" exclaimed Melody. "It's more likely that they're stolen. And it's too late to start making new ones now."

The two older mermaids couldn't conceal their smiles.

"So this year, everyone will be laughing at you, not us," said Myrtle. And still smiling, they swam off.

Melody was furious. "We've just got to get the chest back," she said. "Myrtle's right: Everyone will laugh at us."

"But how?" asked Coral.

"Well, looking at the clues," said Melody, "I'm pretty sure I know who's taken it."

"You do?" said Rosa, surprised.

"It's the sea dragon," Melody announced firmly. "He's the only creature in Mermaid Bay that is big and strong enough to have picked up the chest. He must have broken the coral when he flapped his wings to swim off."

The others were shocked.

"The sea dragon? But you said he had been banished for years and that the water fairies had cast a spell on him. He can't escape, can he?"

"Well, maybe the magic's worn off. And anyway, there's no other explanation for it. The sea dragon is obviously making nighttime outings around the bay and taking for himself whatever he can find. Sea dragons love jewels."

The mermaids had to admit—it did all make sense.

"But what about this?" said Sula, holding up the curious object she had found.

"Oh, that's probably been there for

ages," said Melody.

"I don't think it was here yesterday," insisted Sula. "I would have noticed it. It's quite beautiful," she said, twisting it around.

"Well, I think we should all go and search the sea dragon's lair," said Melody.

"But isn't that terribly dangerous?" asked Sula.

"Not if we go at night when he's not there."

"Well . . . I'm not sure," said Sula. "What does everyone else think?"

"How about we go moon-bathing just as we planned and think about it?" said Rosa. "We need to find some more clues. We can't just go around accusing the sea dragon without any real proof. Perhaps we could talk to the Sandman first thing tomorrow. He lives just outside Rainbow Falls and might have seen something."

"But it's so obvious," argued Melody. "I can't believe you can't all see it. It's *got* to be the sea dragon. There is just no one else. I think we should go tonight. Why wait?"

"I'm sure you're right," said Rosa. "I just want to think about it for a while. Is that OK, Melody?"

"Yes, I suppose so," said Melody sulkily. But it wasn't OK. So when the mermaids headed out toward the beach for an evening's moon-bathing, Melody followed behind for a while and then swam away without any of her friends noticing.

As soon as their heads broke the surface of the water, the mermaids looked around carefully. They had to make sure the beach was empty before going ashore.

"All clear," said Coral. "Let's go! I can't wait to soak up all that moonlight. My tail is tingling with the thought."

So the mermaids let the waves float them forward until they were gently

carried onto the shore. Then, flipping onto their bellies, they stretched their tails out behind them and relaxed.

It was then that Sula noticed Melody was missing. "Where's Melody?" she asked. "Didn't she come ashore?"

"She must have slipped off," said Rosa. "Knowing her, she's probably trying to solve the mystery all by herself!"

"Well, she's not going to ruin my fun. This is just wonderful," said Jasmine, flicking her shimmering blue tail back and forth in the soft sand.

"I could lie here all night."

"We can't do that, Jasmine," said Sula. "We need to find Melody. We can't possibly let her face the sea dragon on her own."

Suddenly, the mermaids heard a noise coming from behind a rock.

"What was that?" whispered Rosa. "Someone's there. Quick, everyone: back into the sea," she urged.

CHAPTER 3

The Sea Sprites

"Look, it's the sea sprites," said
Jasmine with a sigh of relief.

From behind the rock came a group
of three sprites walking toward them,
smiling. They had sweet, round faces,
large, watery eyes, and strong bodies.

"We thought it must be mermaids," said Juno, the tallest of the bunch. "All the land folk went home hours ago. Come ashore for a spot of moon-bathing, have you?"

"Hello, Juno. Yes, we have. You nearly frightened us off, though," said Sula.

"No need for that," replied Juno. "Enjoy yourselves—we're spoiled, having the beach all to ourselves each evening."

The sea sprites were tiny creatures who lived on land among the shoreline rocks and caves. Like mermaids, though, they were happiest when in the sea. They also grew fish tails once they hit the water.

"Yes, it is a beautiful beach," said Sula. "There are so many lovely shells."

"And—look at this," said Jasmine, holding up something that looked very much like the object Sula had found on the seabed.

"There are lots of them. What are they?"

"Those? They're feathers," said Bel, another of the sea sprites. "We use them to make clothes. They fall from the sky—from the birds. Look." Bel pointed at a flock of seagulls sitting on the cliffs.

"That's funny. We found one on the seabed earlier today and wondered what it was," said Rosa suspiciously.

"Yes, we came in for a swim, and I was wearing my feather hat," said Juno. "I probably dropped one." The mermaids looked at each other in astonishment. "We were looking for things that we might wear to the Spring Ball," he continued.

"Oh, were you?" said Rosa, indignantly. "And what did you find?"

"Nothing, really," said Bel, wondering why Rosa was so upset. "Well, apart from an old rusty chest. It's awfully heavy, but we managed to drag it back. Trouble is, it's locked and we can't open it."

"It's probably the remains of an ancient shipwreck," said Juno. "We thought it might contain a hoard of jewels. It's in the sea. Do you want to take a look?"

The mermaids could hardly believe what they were hearing. So Melody was wrong. There was a simple explanation, and this was it.

"I think the chest belongs to us," said Rosa. "Melody's got the key on a chain around her neck."

Now it was the sea sprites' turn to look surprised. Quickly, they led the mermaids back into the sea, and there, sure enough, was the chest, with the waves breaking gently around it.

"Thank goodness," the mermaids sighed.

"We can finish our outfits tomorrow morning, and still be ready for the ball in the afternoon," said Rosa. "There's no need to worry anymore."

"But aren't you forgetting something, Rosa?" said Sula. "What about Melody?"

CHAPTER 4

Spellbound

After swimming away from the rest
of the mermaids, Melody had gone
straight to the Underwater Gardens.
She could see no reason to delay the
visit to the sea dragon, and she knew
that the water fairies could tell her

exactly where to find him. Arriving in
front of the huge metal gates, she rang
the bell. It tinkled gently. Before long,
a tiny water fairy fluttered down.

"Queenie," she shouted, "it's
me, Melody."

"Welcome, welcome, my dear,"
replied Queenie. "How lovely to see
you. But what
brings you here
at this late
hour? We
were just
about to
settle down

for some storytelling."

"Yes, I'm sorry to disturb you, Queenie, but I'm in the middle of solving a very important mystery. I wondered if you could give me some information about the sea dragon; then I'll leave you alone."

"Slow down, slow down," said Queenie. "You mermaids, you're always rushing around. Come on in and tell us what's happened."

So Melody swam through the gates into the Underwater Gardens. The plants were just starting to grow, and a fresh, sweet

smell flowed through the water.
Queenie led Melody to a clearing
where the rest of the water fairies were
gathered. When they saw Melody,
they came over to say hello.

"So, my child," said Queenie.

"What is it you want to know?"

"I want to know all about the sea dragon," Melody began. "I know you put a spell on him when he was banished from Mermaid Bay years and years ago, but where exactly is his lair? And does magic wear off? Because I think he's returning at night to steal jewels."

"Well it is true that sea dragons love jewels. They hoard them in their lairs and keep them safe by sitting on them. And it is true that our sea dragon here in Mermaid Bay was banished, but I'm not sure he's quite

the monster he's made out to be,"
said Queenie. She paused, collecting
her thoughts.

"Around thirty years ago, King
Neptune decided the sea dragon
was getting a little too greedy. Jewels
were being stolen from the palace
and that just wouldn't do. So the
king commanded me to put a spell

on him—a spell that was so strong
it could never be broken and would
banish the sea dragon forever."

"Forever. That's a really long time,"
said Melody.

Queenie paused
again. "If I tell
you something,
Melody, you have
to promise never to
tell a soul. It's a water
fairies' secret and I want
to keep it that way."

"I promise," said Melody.

"I agonized for a week over that

command from the king. I thought forever was too long. In the end, I went to see the sea dragon and asked him about the stealing and about the missing mermaid. He told me he had taken a few jewels but nothing else, and that he knew nothing about the missing mermaid. I believed him.

I told him about King Neptune's request, and together we agreed that if I found him a lair in the caves behind Rainbow Falls, he would never return uninvited to Mermaid Bay again. There was no magic spell to keep him there—just his word. The network of tunnels behind Rainbow Falls leads out into the ocean, so the dragon would still have its freedom."

"Which is why there have been sightings of him in recent years," said Melody.

"Exactly," said Queenie, "but not in Mermaid Bay. He promised me he would never return unless invited."

"Well, I'm afraid the temptation of jewels has brought him back," said Melody. "He's stolen all of ours."

"Are you sure it's him?" asked Queenie doubtfully.

"Absolutely—all the clues point to

him. Only the sea dragon could have stolen them."

"Well," said Queenie, "perhaps it's time to pay him another visit. Perhaps I will have to use that spell after all."

So Melody, Queenie, and the other water fairies all set off for Rainbow Falls.

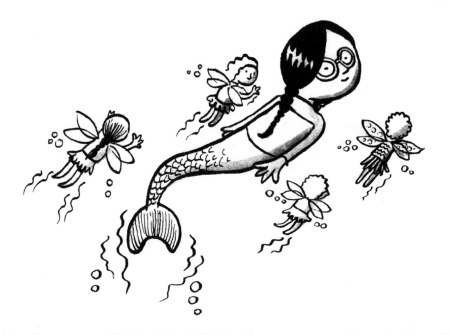

CHAPTER 5

Melody's Mistake

As Melody and the water fairies were swimming toward Rainbow Falls, Rosa, Coral, Jasmine, and Sula were saying their good-byes to the water sprites.

"Once we've found Melody, we'll be

right back with the key to the chest," said Rosa.

"We're sorry we've caused you so much trouble," said Juno. "We really thought it had been abandoned."

"Don't worry," said Sula. "At least we've got it back now."

Soon the four mermaids were on their way to find Melody. "Where shall we look first?" said Jasmine. "She said something about the water fairies. We could visit them."

"That's a good idea," said Rosa. So off they swam to the Underwater Gardens. They pulled the bell and, just like it had for Melody, it tinkled gently. Only this time no one appeared.

"That's strange," said Rosa. "The water fairies are always here."

"We could try the Merschool," said Jasmine. "Perhaps she's in the library reading up on the sea dragon."

"Good idea," replied Rosa. "Let's go. I hope we can find her."

But when they got to the Merschool, it was dark inside. "She can't be here," said Coral. "It's locked up for the night. Where now?"

"Well, what about Myrtle and Muriel?" said Sula. "They might know where she is." So the young mermaids went to the older mermaids' cavern. There, they found Myrtle and Muriel sewing sea stars onto their cloaks.

"We're just about ready," said Muriel. "And you? Have you found your outfits yet?"

"Sort of," said Jasmine.

"What do you mean, 'sort of'?" said Myrtle.

"Surely either you have or you haven't?"

"Well, we've found the chest, but we've lost Melody, and she's got the key," said Sula. "Have you seen her?"

The two mermaids laughed. "And why should we tell you? Especially after what happened at the Spring Ball last year."

Rosa was furious. She opened her mouth to say something, but Coral

spoke instead. "Come on, Rosa. It's not worth arguing with them. What about visiting the Sandman? He usually knows what's going on in Mermaid Bay."

So the four friends rushed off toward Sandman's Shop, which was just outside Rainbow Falls.

The Sandman was Mermaid Bay's oldest resident. Some say he had once married a mermaid, exchanging his life on land for a life forever in the sea. Others said he came from somewhere far away called Atlantis, where humans lived beneath the waves. All the mermaids knew was that he had a cavern full of curious and useful objects, which he allowed them to borrow from time to time. In return, they brought him food.

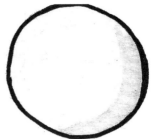

When they arrived, he was sitting outside in his rocking chair, playing his water pipe so that a trail of musical bubbles floated above his head.

"Hello there, girls," he called as they swam up to him. "And what can I do for you this fine evening? All set for the ball?"

"Hello, Sandman. Well, no, we're not ready, actually," replied Rosa. "We need to find Melody. You haven't seen her, have you?"

"As a matter of fact, I have," he answered. "She passed by here about ten minutes ago, surrounded by a flutter of water fairies. She waved before heading through Rainbow Falls."

The mermaids looked aghast.

"That means she's going to accuse the sea dragon of stealing," said Jasmine, "but she's got it all wrong. He'll be furious. Goodness knows

what he'll do. If only she'd waited like
we asked her to . . ."

CHAPTER 6

The Sea Dragon's Surprise

The four mermaids thanked the Sandman and quickly set off toward the cascade at Rainbow Falls. Huge bubbles rolled around the surging water, and the mermaids were thrown this way and that as they swam

through. In front of them was a
dark tunnel.

Rosa sped ahead of the others,
desperate to find Melody.
Onward she
swam, until
she finally saw a
faint light glowing
in the distance.
Soon it shone in a
bright stream. At the
end of the tunnel was
a huge underwater cave
lit up with sunlight,
which poured through its

ceiling. Inside, there was the biggest pile of jewels she had ever seen.

"Oh no!" Rosa exclaimed. Following closely behind, the other mermaids gasped, too. There, in the middle of the cavern, lying on the floor, was Melody. Standing over her with its huge leathery wings, bright green scales, and long, sharp teeth was the sea dragon. High above them, flitting nervously about, were the water fairies.

Bravely Rosa swam over. "What happened?" she asked. The sea dragon and the water fairies looked surprised—

they hadn't seen the mermaids enter the cavern.

"Oh, Rosa," said Queenie, "thank goodness you've arrived. Melody is under a spell. She sprinkled her magic sand over the sea dragon while reciting the words to put him in a trance, but he sneezed, and it ended up all over her instead. We didn't bring any with us, so we can't reverse the spell and wake her up."

"I've got some magic sand here in my purse," said Coral. "We could use that."

"Wonderful," said Queenie. She

sprinkled
it over
Melody's
head. Melody
rubbed her eyes
and yawned.

"What happened?"
said Melody, slowly waking up. "What
are you doing here?"

"We came to find you," said Rosa.
"The sea dragon didn't take our chest.
The sea sprites have it."

"The sea sprites? But what about the
clues?"

"Oh dear," said Queenie. "I should

have stopped you. I always believed
the sea dragon would keep his promise
never to return to Mermaid Bay—
unless, of course, he was invited."

"And I should have listened to you
all," said Melody. "I'm sorry."

"Never mind," said Rosa, forgiving
her friend instantly.
"Let's go back to the
beach and unlock
the chest."

They turned to say
good-bye to the water
fairies, and as they did,
they noticed the sea

dragon looked rather sad.

"It must be terrible," said Sula, "spending your life alone, banished from the one place you really love."

"Yes. I suppose all the jewels in the world can't make up for not having

any friends," said Melody.

And rather thoughtfully, the mermaids swam back through the tunnel toward Mermaid Bay.

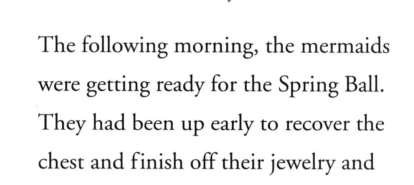

The following morning, the mermaids were getting ready for the Spring Ball. They had been up early to recover the chest and finish off their jewelry and

clothes. Everyone was more than happy with their outfits.

"That's an amazing tiara, Sula," said

Jasmine, "and your top matches the
color of your tail."

"Thank you, Jasmine. I made the
tiara using opals and sea stars, and
the top is just strips of
knotted seagrass. I
wove sea stars into
the straps to make
it sparkle."

"And your coral
headdress, Rosa, is
beautiful," Sula continued. "Where
did you find that sea fan?"

"The water fairies gave me that
last night," said Rosa. "They've been

growing it all year especially for me."

"Well, everyone looks amazing," said Coral. "Are we ready?"

"I'm sorry about the water ponies," said Rosa. "With all the excitement yesterday, there just wasn't time to magic them up."

"Don't worry, Rosa," said Jasmine. "We can swim there. In fact, we should get going. We don't want to be late."

"Where's Melody? She should be here by now," said Rosa.

Just then there was a shout. "Rosa, Coral, Jasmine, Sula—look at me!" The mermaids spun around to see Melody sitting majestically on the back of the sea dragon. Its large wings were flapping in the water, carrying her toward them at high speed.

"Melody," shouted Rosa, "what

in the water are you doing? The sea
dragon's not allowed here."

"But he is!" shouted Melody.
"I got up early and swam out to King
Neptune's Palace. I explained about
my mistake and asked him to imagine
how lonely the sea dragon must have

been for all these years."

"And he listened to you?" said Sula in disbelief.

"Yes!" exclaimed Melody. "More than that, he's invited the sea dragon to the Spring Ball. So what are you waiting for? Jump up."

The mermaids could hardly believe it. No one had ever arrived at the ball on a dragon before! So the four mermaids climbed onto his back and held on very tightly. Soon the sea dragon was flapping his enormous wings, and the mermaids were flying swiftly toward Watery Downs.

"You know what?" shouted Melody.
"What?" replied her mermaid
friends.

"Sea dragons are the oldest species in the sea. They have been—"

But Melody didn't get to finish her sentence. The mermaids all opened their mouths and started singing at the tops of their voices. "OK," said Melody, laughing. "I know how to take a hint!" And she sang along with them, too.

Mermaid Mysteries

There's a mystery to be solved—and the young mermaid detectives are on the case!

Mermaid Mysteries

Rosa and the **Water Pony**

Katy Kit   Illustrated by Tom Knight

Mermaid Mysteries

Jasmine and the **Treasure Chest**

Katy Kit   Illustrated by Tom Knight

ZAPATO POWER: THE ADVENTURES OF FREDDIE RAMOS

One day Freddie Ramos comes home
from school and finds a strange box
just for him. What's inside?